W9-AQK-317

# GOOD D🐾G 4

## Fireworks Night

by
Cam Higgins

illustrated by
Ariel Landy

LITTLE SIMON

New York  London  Toronto  Sydney  New Delhi

This book is a work of fiction. Any references to historical events, real people, or real places are used fictitiously. Other names, characters, places, and events are products of the author's imagination, and any resemblance to actual events or places or persons, living or dead, is entirely coincidental.

LITTLE SIMON
An imprint of Simon & Schuster Children's Publishing Division
1230 Avenue of the Americas, New York, New York 10020
First Little Simon hardcover edition May 2021
Copyright © 2021 by Simon & Schuster, Inc.
Also available in a Little Simon paperback edition.
All rights reserved, including the right of reproduction in whole or in part in any form. LITTLE SIMON is a registered trademark of Simon & Schuster, Inc., and associated colophon is a trademark of Simon & Schuster, Inc.
For information about special discounts for bulk purchases, please contact Simon & Schuster Special Sales at 1-866-506-1949 or business@simonandschuster.com.
The Simon & Schuster Speakers Bureau can bring authors to your live event. For more information or to book an event contact the Simon & Schuster Speakers Bureau at 1-866-248-3049 or visit our website at www.simonspeakers.com.
Designed by Leslie Mechanic
Manufactured in the United States of America 0421 FFG
10 9 8 7 6 5 4 3 2 1
Library of Congress Cataloging-in-Publication Data
Names: Higgins, Cam, author. | Landy, Ariel, illustrator.
Title: Fireworks night / by Cam Higgins; illustrated by Ariel Landy.
Description: First Little Simon paperback edition. | New York: Little Simon, 2021. | Series: Good dog; 4 | Audience: Ages 5–9. |
Summary: After learning about fireworks from Nanny Sheep, farm pup Bo reassures his best canine friend Scrapper that fireworks are not evil monsters.
Identifiers: LCCN 2020051540 (print) | LCCN 2020051541 (eBook) | ISBN 9781534495326 (hardcover) | ISBN 9781534495319 (paperback) | ISBN 9781534495333 (eBook)
Subjects: CYAC: Dogs—Fiction. | Animals—Infancy—Fiction. | Best friends—Fiction. | Friendship—Fiction. | Fireworks—Fiction. | Farm life—Fiction.
Classification: LCC PZ7.1.H54497 Fi 2021 (print) | LCC PZ7.1.H54497 (eBook) | DDC [Fic]—dc23
LC record available at https://lccn.loc.gov/2020051540

# CONTENTS

# Scrapper

You might not think that puppies are the kind of animals who are interested in secret forts, but guess what? We totally are!

This is Scrapper. He's my best dog friend. He lives one house over from the Davis farm.

There's a forest in between our homes, and we love to play there. But not today. Today we were playing at Scrapper's house.

Scrapper has three humans in his family. There's Tom and Rey and their son, Hank. Hank's a really great kid, but more importantly, he's an amazing ball-thrower.

Humans might not understand why
dogs like to play fetch so much. But
honestly, I can't see how it's so different
from two people playing catch.

Only, fetch is better! You get to run all over the place and catch the ball—or stick or Frisbee—in your mouth. Then you get to chew and slobber all over it!

What's not to love about that? Humans should try it sometime.

Plus, if it weren't for fetch, Scrapper and I would have never discovered our secret dog fort!

You see, we were playing a special game of fetch. Hank had a brand-new bouncy ball. How bouncy was it? It was faster and bouncier than any ball I'd ever seen. On Hank's first toss, that ball flew deep into the woods, and Scrapper and I chased after it.

That ball rolled past rocks, flew off roots, and sprang over fallen tree trunks.

When it finally slowed down, guess where it had landed? Right in front of a small, gray, bushy-tailed squirrel!

Now, what was a dog supposed to do when he had to choose between a ball and a squirrel?

I froze. Scrapper paused. But that squirrel sure knew what to do.

He kicked the ball as hard as he could with both his feet and sent it flying even deeper into the forest.

And then he took off running, hopping away as fast as he could go.

Scrapper and I looked at each other.
There was only one choice.

I mean, we could chase squirrels
anytime—there were so many of them
in the woods. But there was only one
wonderful mega bouncy ball that we
knew of. And we had to catch it!

Panting and feeling the wind whooshing through our fur, we dashed between trees and leaped over logs searching for that ball.

Finally, Scrapper and I skidded to a stop when we found it nestled in a bed of moss to the side of a pile of fallen trees. I went after the ball, but Scrapper was looking at something else.

# Summer
# Days

I turned to see what Scrapper had found. He was sniffing at the base of the tree.

Suddenly, he stood on his hind legs and pushed on one of the tree trunks with his front paw.

"Waaa ah ooo oooing?" I asked.

But Scrapper couldn't understand me.

It's hard to talk with a ball gripped between your teeth.

I set the ball down and tried again. "What are you doing?"

"I'm discovering!" Scrapper yipped excitedly.

"Discovering what?" I asked. "A stack of old wood?"

I could not figure out why Scrapper's tail was wagging so happily. Clearly, I was missing something.

Scrapper poked his head into a narrow gap between two tree trunks. Then the rest of him followed and he disappeared! Oh, no! That tree ate my friend!

I pounced against that tree with my paws and barked as loud as I could!

"Calm down, Bo!" a voice echoed from inside the tree.

*Hmm, that voice sounded a lot like Scrapper,* I thought.

Then my best friend burst from between the trees with a humongous smile on his face.

"Bo! You have to see this! It's our new puppy fort!" he shouted. "Come with me and check it out!"

Phew! So I guess trees don't eat dogs. I felt very happy about that . . . and a little silly for thinking they might.

Scrapper waved me over with a nod of his head and darted back inside the fort.

First I picked up the ball because
you never know what evil plots those
squirrels might be hatching. Then I
stepped through to the dark shadows
between the trees.

It was cool inside the circle of trees, which felt nice. Summer days at the farm could be awfully hot, even in the shade.

A little bit of light shined through the roof formed by tree branches and leaves above us. This meant we still could easily see all around us.

"It's great, right?" Scrapper asked. "We can use this as our secret hideout while looking for *you-know-what!*"

I wish I could say that Scrapper wanted to search for squirrels. But I knew he was talking about keeping watch for his monster.

Scrapper was certain that there was a monster living in this forest. He even thought he had seen it before. I wasn't so sure, but Scrapper was my best friend. And best friends help each other out, even if it means hunting monsters.

"That sounds like a plan," I said, "but we better get back before Hank doesn't want to play fetch anymore."

"Good idea," Scrapper agreed. "But first let's mark our fort so we know how to find it tonight!"

Do you know how dogs leave their mark? Well, let me tell you—it isn't pretty.

# Summer
# Nights

Summer days on the farm were hot, but summer nights were nice and cool.

After dinner, I stepped outside and felt the breeze ruffling my fur. It was soft and comforting, like an old friend.

The sky glowed purple and orange as the sun began to dip behind the trees. I headed for the forest to meet Scrapper.

He was waiting for me in front of the fort with a bag.

"First order of dog business, this place needs a name," Scrapper said. "I vote for Camp Monster-Finder."

I thought that was a pretty good name. It said what it was.

"Oh, and I brought stuff that monsters like," Scrapper told me.

He nuzzled open the bag and flipped it upside down. There was a yummy-looking bone, a comic book that I guessed belonged to Hank, some glow-in-the-dark toys, and a monster mask.

"Won't you get in trouble for taking these things?" I asked.

"Oh, I'll bring them back later," said Scrapper. "Besides, Hank never plays with these anymore. This comic book has been under his bed for weeks. And he hasn't worn the mask in a year."

I sniffed at the mask. It was pretty weird-looking. "Do you think the mask might scare away the monster?"

"Bo," Scrapper said with a chuckle. "You just don't understand monsters the way I do. They are very curious creatures. If they see another monster, they're going to want to come over to see what it's doing."

"But what about the comic book? Can monsters even read?" I asked doubtfully.

Scrapper thought about that one.

"They can look at the pictures," he answered. "Plus, monsters need toys that glow to play with, because they come out at night. And I brought the bone in case the monster gets hungry. We all know a bone is great to chew on."

*Hmmm.* Scrapper was making a lot of sense!

We scattered the supplies on the ground and in the bushes outside the fort, and then we went to wait inside.

The night was quiet, and it was getting late. Even the squirrels were asleep by now. Just as my eyelids were starting to grow heavy, it happened.

There was a very loud, whistling SCREECH followed by a thundering BOOM that echoed above us.

Scrapper and I jumped from the
fort and looked up just in time to see
a shower of sizzling lights in the sky.

They snapped and popped and fizzed
their way right down toward us.

"It's the MONSTER!" Scrapper yelled.
And that was all we needed to know.
It was time to go, go, go!

# Mean Cats Kitten Around

Running through a dark forest at night with an angry monster exploding above us was not fun. Not fun at all.

But Scrapper and I were fast. We hightailed it to my house, then skidded to a sudden stop on the front path.

Those pesky barn cats, King and Diva, were lying on the porch. It was like they had been waiting for us.

"What's the rush, little pups?" Diva hissed with a wicked grin. "You look so frightened! Is there a big scary squirrel chasing you?"

"This is no time for jokes, Diva!" Scrapper howled. "There is a monster after us!"

Another burst of light exploded in the sky with a loud bang.

"See!" I yelped.

But those barn cats didn't flinch or look scared at all. They just rolled over onto their backs and started laughing their whiskers off.

"Hey, it's not funny!" Scrapper said.

"Oh, you silly pups," said King. "Those lights in the sky aren't a monster."

"Huh. What are they, then?" I asked.

King sat up and started to clean his paws. He licked between each sharp claw. "Those are just stars," he said.

"I've never seen stars that do that," said Scrapper.

"Pups, don't you know stars explode when they're angry?" Diva asked. "And the stars must be very angry with you, Scrapper!"

He looked terrified, and his tail drooped between his legs.

"But why? What did I do wrong?" he cried.

That's when Imani and Wyatt, my human sister and brother, stepped out onto the porch. The screen door slammed shut behind them with a loud crack that startled the cats.

Diva and King hopped to their feet and slunk away faster than a pup could snatch a scrap of food that fell under the dinner table.

Unfortunately, the loud noise also scared Scrapper off. He darted away before I could even say good-bye.

"Bo! I'm so glad you're here," said Imani as she waved me over.

I bounded up the steps and leaped into her arms. I was really scared, and it felt good to be held when I was frightened.

Wyatt gave me a soft pat too. "Poor Bo, you are shaking! Are you scared? I bet it was the fireworks. They can be upsetting with all that noise."

"Don't worry, Bo," Imani said, planting a kiss on my head. "You're safe. This is just a little practice for the big show tomorrow night.

We'll make sure we stay with you
when the real fireworks go off."

Imani carried me inside and set me
down. Now I was wondering what in
the world they were talking about.

# What's a Firework?

The next morning my human parents, Darnell and Jennica, were busy in the kitchen.

I could smell all kinds of good food cooking: biscuits, cookies, beans, corn, potatoes. I also spied piles of hot dogs and plates of uncooked hamburger patties in the fridge.

This was way more food than the Davis family usually ate. I wondered what was going on.

I joined Wyatt and Imani for chore time.

While they fed the pigs, I asked my good friend Zonks if today was a special farm day or something.

Zonks thought for a moment, then said, "I don't think so. But there is one animal who would know."

He didn't even have to say another word. I knew just the animal to ask.

I trotted out to the field and found Nanny Sheep talking to a flock of lambs. I sat down next to them in the grass.

"My dear lamb friends," Nanny Sheep began. "And my puppy friend, too. Tonight is a very special night for the humans. This year the Davis family is having a party for their friends. They will eat lots of food, and they will be happy and very noisy. And then, when it gets dark, there will be a fireworks show."

Oh, I sat up even straighter and raised my paw. I had heard that word before!

"Fireworks? What are those?" I barked.

"Fireworks are special lights that humans send up into the night sky," Nanny Sheep explained. "The lights glow and spin and spark and shine. But they also make a very loud sound.

You may have heard or seen the fireworks last night."

Several of the lambs looked around at one another and nodded.

One young lamb jumped to his feet and baaed. "I heard them, and I was so scared!"

I woofed in agreement. I had felt the same way last night!

Another lamb puffed out his wool. "I was afraid too!"

The lambs all began nodding and baaing. I guess Scrapper and I weren't the only animals freaked out by the fireworks.

Nanny Sheep gently hushed us. "Yes, my young ones, fireworks can certainly be surprising, especially when we are used to the stars shining quietly in the sky. But for humans this

is a very special night, and they like to celebrate. So, just remember that although fireworks are noisy, they are supposed to be fun and make everyone smile."

Oh boy, I felt so much better now!
Leave it to Nanny Sheep to calm
everybody down and explain exactly
what needed explaining.

I couldn't wait to tell Scrapper. He didn't have to feel sad or scared anymore either. Those barn cats were just teasing him last night.

For now, though, I could hear Wyatt calling me back home.

A pup's work is never done.

# All the Smells

Later that day the party started. First a few people arrived, and then more and more trickled into the yard. I had never seen so many cars and trucks parked at the farm.

And with every new visitor came a new tray of food! And believe me, it smelled yummy!

I imagined what it would be like if all those humans were bringing all that tasty food just for me. That was a yummy tummy daydream!

Finally, a truck that I knew all too well pulled through the gates. It was Scrapper's family! I ran over to greet them with happy barks, but when the doors opened, only Hank and his parents stepped out. Where was Scrapper?

I must have looked really confused, because Hank leaned down and patted my head.

"Hi, Bo," he said. "Are you looking for Scrapper?"

I gave a yip and spun around in a circle.

Hank let out a laugh. "Aww, I'm so sorry, Bo. Scrapper stayed home. Something scared him pretty bad last  night. It was probably the fireworks, but just in case, we didn't want him to come to the party and get scared.

So we're just going to be here until the fireworks begin. Then we'll go home to make sure he's all right."

I was impressed. Hank was such a thoughtful dog owner and an all-around great human. I gave him a lick, then led him over to the backyard, where the party was in full swing.

Being a dog at a party is *never* boring. There is so much to see, and lots to hear, of course. And then there are *all the smells*.

Sure, there's always amazing food, but the people at a party have lots of different scents too! Some wear perfume, some, um . . . don't. Some  humans smell like candy or cookies or meat. Others can smell like coffee— mainly just the

grown-up humans. No matter what, they all smell interesting.

As the party went on, the sky grew darker. Luckily, the Davis family had outside lights set up. When they switched on, it was magical.

The other great thing about this party was that people ate outside. And outside eating means they use paper plates. And do you know what happens when people eat using paper plates? Food spills on the ground.

And guess what else? Humans almost never eat food that falls on the ground. And when they're outdoors, they usually don't even pick it up. Do you know who does? DOGS!

And I was the only dog around.

I found chips. I found vegetables and cookies and cake crumbs. I found hot dog buns. I even found half a hot dog! What a night!

I was so busy sniffing around that I found a smell I wasn't expecting at all hiding under a picnic table. It was Scrapper!

"Hey!" I cried. "What are you doing here? Hank said you were staying at home."

"Do I look like the kind of dog who stays at home, Bo?" he said. "No. No, I don't. I'm a party dog. And do you know what I am here to do, Bo?"

"Um . . . party?" I guessed.

"You know it!" he cheered. "Now, let's find the man in the brown boots. He's carrying a baby who keeps throwing food on the ground. It's amazing!"

I laughed. Scrapper was such a smart dog when it came to finding food scraps. Maybe that was why they called him Scrapper?

We found the man in the brown boots who was holding the baby, and sure enough, that kid didn't want to eat anything! Which of course meant that Scrapper and I ate everything.

With our bellies full, I didn't think
the night could get any better.
And I was right.

# Color
# Sky

"Okay, friends, it's fireworks time!" Darnell announced excitedly.

The crowd sat on blankets in the lawn, and everybody looked up in the sky.

Everyone except Hank's family. I saw their truck driving back to their house.

"Fireworks? What are those?" asked Scrapper. "They sound fancy."

Oh, no! We were so busy hunting for food that I'd forgotten to let Scrapper know what Nanny Sheep had told us about fireworks!

I tried to warn him, but it was too late.

The night sky exploded with color. Whistles and booms echoed across the countryside, with bangs so loud I thought the sky was cracking open.

It didn't matter that I knew we were safe.
Scrapper didn't! He whined loudly and tore
off into the woods.

I chased after him, but Scrapper has

always been much faster than I am. And the dark did not make things easier. I ran as quickly as I could, trying to catch up to him.

"Scrapper!" I shouted between the blasts of the fireworks. "Scrapper, hey, it's okay!"

The noise was so loud. There was no way he would ever hear me. I panted, squinting my eyes to try to see through the trees.

Another blast of fireworks filled the air. Even I had a hard time believing everything was okay when the sky was busy with such loud thunder and lights.

When I made it to Scrapper's house,
I scratched at the door with my paw
and barked loudly.

Hank opened the door immediately.
He looked very worried.

"Bo! Have you seen Scrapper? He isn't here!" Hank sounded even more upset than he looked.

Uh-oh. If Scrapper wasn't home, where was he?

"Bo! Have you seen Scrapper? He isn't here!" Hank sounded even more upset than he looked.

Uh-oh. If Scrapper wasn't home, where was he?

# Scary or
# Very Scary

Another firework lit up the night and sizzled over the forest.

Hey, the forest! Suddenly I knew exactly where to find my best pup friend. I left Hank and charged into the trees.

The forest was a little scary at night, but I reminded myself that there was nothing to worry about.

I headed straight for our fort. Well, as straight as one could go in a forest at night.

Scrapper *had* to be at Camp Monster-Finder. It was the only answer!

As the fireworks whizzed and boomed brightly above the trees, the shadows in the forest lit up briefly before darkness quickly swept back over them.

The lights played tricks on my eyes. Every stump turned into Scrapper's monster. Tree branches looked like claws reaching toward me.

Okay, I was wrong. The forest was actually VERY scary at night. But I was on a mission, and I couldn't back out. I woofed and ran faster.

Then I stopped. I didn't want to be
afraid anymore, so I closed my eyes
and tried to use my nose to pick up
Scrapper's scent.

I took a deep breath. The whole forest smelled like rotten eggs for some reason. Maybe it had something to do with the fireworks?

Finally, I caught Scrapper's scent and ran toward our fort!

Oh, I was so happy when I found it that I howled with joy. Then I saw something glowing in a bush next to the fort. They looked like eyes . . . and they were watching me!

"Scrapper?" I whispered. "Scrapper, is that you?"

The glowing eyes blinked at the sound of my voice. Then they started moving toward me. My heart raced, but I was not going anywhere without my friend.

I don't know what came over me, but I jumped up on my hind legs and let out the deepest bark I could. Luckily, a firework went off at the same time, and it made my bark go BOOM!

And it worked! The glowing eyes scrambled all around like scaredy little squirrels. That's because they were squirrels! Squirrels playing with the glow toys Scrapper had brought to the fort.

I let out a great big sigh of relief.

That's when something else jumped out of the fort. It had the body of a dog with the terrible, horrible head of . . . a MONSTER!

# Brave
# Puppy

"Woof, woof, woof, woof!" the monster barked at the squirrels. They dropped the toys and raced off into the forest faster than a squirrel had ever run.

*Please be a nice monster! Please be a nice monster!* was all I could think.

The beast stopped barking and turned to face me.

As its big, ugly head swiveled in my direction, I felt my doggy heart pound. Then the monster spoke. "Are you okay, Bo?"

I knew that voice! It was Scrapper! He shook his head, and the monster mask flew off. I've never been so happy to see Scrapper's big grin.

"Did you see those silly squirrels? I really fooled them!" Scrapper boasted.

"You fooled me, too!" I screamed.

"Aw, I'm sorry about that," said Scrapper. He looked up at the sky, suddenly nervous. "Hey, uh, we should go before the stars get angry again."

"The stars?" I said. "Oh, those aren't stars. They're fireworks, and have I got news for you!"

First I told Scrapper that he should never, ever trust the word of a barn cat. They were only interested in making trouble. Then I told him that fireworks weren't supposed to be scary.

"They're flashes of light that the humans make to celebrate. Tonight is some sort of big deal for humans," I explained. "So to celebrate it, they bring color at night."

"Really?" Scrapper asked.

"Really!" I said. "All the humans are back at my farm watching the sky and cheering."

"Gosh, Bo," said Scrapper as he looked at the ground with his tail drooping. "You must think I'm the silliest scaredy-cat pup ever."

I shook my head. "No way, Scrapper! Even during the scary fireworks, you left the fort to rescue me from those squirrels. I think that makes you one of the bravest pups I know! And my very best friend."

Scrapper wagged his tail and said, "You know what, Bo? Now that I think about it, you're right! Plus, you came looking for me and stood up to those squirrels—which means you're my very best friend too."

I held out my paw and said, "Best friends forever?"

Scrapper slapped his paw down on mine. "Totally! Now let's go back to my house and watch the rest of the angry stars before they go back to sleep."

# Fireworks Night

When Hank saw Scrapper, he wrapped him up in a great big hug!

Then the three of us sat on the porch watching the rest of the fireworks show. Hank even gave us some cookie treats that tasted like chicken. Yum!

That was our first Fireworks Night, but it wouldn't be the last.

In fact, there were lots more, and let me tell you—we always ate well! One time a whole pie fell on the ground, and we got to eat the entire thing. Okay, maybe the pie had a little help falling down to the ground. But no one was any the wiser, and it was worth it.

Another time, King and Diva tried to play a practical joke on us, but it totally backfired.

See, they wanted Scrapper and me to stand under a table so they could dump a bowl full of punch on us. But when a firework exploded in the sky, it scared those cats so bad, they lost their balance. And do you know where they landed? Right in the punch bowl!

You should have seen it! They looked so funny, soaked to their barn-cat bones. Scrapper and I laughed so hard, our sides started to hurt!

Oh, and once, Hank had a sleepover with Wyatt, which meant Scrapper got to spend the night too! We stayed awake almost all night long, watching the fireworks, then listening to Hank and Wyatt tell ghost stories.

Plus, they shared their snacks with us. Scrapper and I even got to try some marshmallows when the boys made hot cocoa. How cool is that?

So now Scrapper and I look forward to Fireworks Night every year. But I will never ever forget our very first Fireworks Night. Because that's the night we became best friends forever.

Here's a peek at Bo's next big adventure!

GOOD D🐾G

The Swimming Hole

Every farm has a big tree.

You know, a huge one with wide limbs perfect for human kids to climb. One that you can't miss.

Sometimes the tree is next to the barn. Sometimes it's in front of the house.

An excerpt from *The Swimming Hole*

The big tree on our farm is in the middle of the field. And during the hottest days of summer, everyone gathers there.

*Why?* you might ask. Because the big tree gives the absolute coolest, best shade.

Every animal on the farm needs shade on hot summer days. The cats stay in the barn, horses stay in their stalls, and pigs stay in the mud—if they are lucky enough to find a pool of mud.

But when it is so hot that it feels like the sun is tapping you on the back, the best place to be is under the big tree.

An excerpt from *The Swimming Hole*

All the animals meet there, and it's like a party. Well, it's more like a slumber party, because everybody likes to close their eyes and enjoy the sweet breeze.

One sunny day, a young bird perched in the branches of the big tree and began singing.

I liked his song. It went like this: "Tweetly tweet tweet, sweetly tweet tweet twee."

Billy the goat, on the other hand, did not like the song. He did not like it at all.